Karen's Figure Eight

**Other books by
Ann M. Martin**

P. S. Longer Letter Later
(written with Paula Danziger)
Leo the Magnificat
Rachel Parker, Kindergarten Show-off
Eleven Kids, One Summer
Ma and Pa Dracula
Yours Turly, Shirley
Ten Kids, No Pets
With You and Without You
Me and Katie (the Pest)
Stage Fright
Inside Out
Bummer Summer

For older readers:

Missing Since Monday
Just a Summer Romance
Slam Book

THE BABY-SITTERS CLUB series
THE BABY-SITTERS CLUB mysteries
THE KIDS IN MS. COLMAN'S CLASS series
BABY-SITTERS LITTLE SISTER series
(see inside book covers for a complete listing)

Little Sister

Karen's Figure Eight
Ann M. Martin

Illustrations by Susan Crocca Tang

A
LITTLE APPLE
PAPERBACK

SCHOLASTIC INC.
New York Toronto London Auckland Sydney
Mexico City New Delhi Hong Kong

ISBN 0-590-52498-4

12 11 10 9 8 7 6 5 4 3 2 1   0 1 2 3 4 5/0

Printed in the U.S.A.   40
First Scholastic printing, February 2000

The author gratefully acknowledges
Helen Perelman
for her help
with this book.

Karen's Figure Eight

1

Mail for Me!

I love getting mail. And I especially love getting mail in February. That is when I get lots of valentines. And I, Karen Brewer, love Valentine's Day too.

When I got home from school I ran to our front hall to look at the mail. I saw lots of envelopes. And I spotted a red envelope with my name on it! I looked at the return address. It was from Granny in Nebraska. Granny is my grandmother.

Granny's card was a valentine. On the

front of it was a picture of a bunch of grapes with smiling faces. I read the inside of the card out loud. (I am a very good reader.)

You are the sweetest one in the bunch
Happy Valentine's Day
   Love, Granny

Then Andrew came into the hall. (Andrew is my little brother. He is four going on five.) Granny sent Andrew a card too. Andrew's card was in the shape of a racing car. It said:

You always come in first place with me.
Happy Valentine's Day!
   Love, Granny

Andrew and I were about to show Mommy our valentines when I saw another red envelope. My name was printed on the label, but it did not look like a valentine. I opened it anyway, just in case. Inside was a shiny brochure from the Stoneybrook Ice Arena. Blue letters across the top said ICE SKATING LESSONS FOR THE WHOLE FAMILY! A few skaters were pictured doing spins on the ice. Andrew did not seem interested. But I wanted to spin just like them.

"Mommy, Mommy! Look at this!" I shouted.

Mommy looked up from stringing beads. She was working on a new necklace. "Karen, please use your indoor voice."

(Sometimes I forget to use my indoor voice. Ms. Colman, my teacher, is always reminding me to use it too.)

I handed the brochure to Mommy. "Look! I want to do that," I said more quietly. "I want to take skating lessons at the Stoneybrook Ice Arena."

As Mommy read the brochure, I took off my shoes so I could slide around the living room floor as if I were skating on the ice. Andrew started to laugh and joined me. (He likes to do things that I do.) Then I remem-

bered a song that Granny taught me about ice skating.

"Ice skating is nice skating,
But there is one thing about ice skating —
Never skate where the ice is thin.
Thin ice will crack
And you will fall right in
And come up with icicles under your chin
If you skate where the ice is thin!"

"Oh, Mommy," I said as I twirled on my socks. "I would love to take lessons."

"Karen," Mommy said. "The lessons are Wednesday, Friday, and Saturday afternoons. That is a lot of time. Do you *really* want to take lessons?" Mommy asked.

"Yes!" I said. "And I can use the new ice skates that Granny gave me for Christmas."

Mommy asked Andrew if he wanted to take lessons, but he was not interested.

"All right," Mommy said. "I will call now and see if we can get you started soon."

"That is great!" I said. "Maybe the Musketeers would like to take lessons too."

The Three Musketeers are my two best friends, Nancy Dawes and Hannie Papadakis, and I. I will tell you more about them later.

I called my friends right away. But Nancy had dance class on Wednesdays, and Hannie had piano lessons on Fridays. Boo and bullfrogs. The Three Musketeers could not skate together.

I could not stop thinking about my lessons. Maybe I would get to be in an ice-skating show. I would be gigundoly excited about skating for an audience. But I would need lots of tickets if my whole family wanted to come. That is because my family is really *two* families. Hold on a minute and I will explain.

2

My Family

I have two families because my mommy and daddy divorced when I was little. Even though they loved Andrew and me, they did not love each other anymore. The four of us used to live in the house that Daddy grew up in. After the divorce, Mommy, Andrew, and I moved to another house in Stoneybrook. Andrew and I call it the little house because it is smaller than Daddy's big house.

The three of us were living in the little house when Mommy met a man named

7

Seth Engle. He is a carpenter and he is really nice. He loves animals. He has a dog named Midgie and a cat named Rocky. When Mommy and Seth married, Seth and his pets moved into the little house with us.

Then my daddy got married again too. Elizabeth, my stepmother, is super-nice. She has four kids. Charlie and Sam are so old they are in high school. Kristy (the world's best baby-sitter *and* big sister) is in eighth grade. And David Michael is seven just like me. (But he goes to a different school than I do.) Then Elizabeth and Daddy adopted Emily Michelle from Vietnam. She is two and a half and very cute. I even named my pet rat after her. I think Emily Michelle looks up to me.

Nannie also lives in the big house. (She is Elizabeth's mommy.) She came to stay once Emily Michelle arrived. She is a great cook and even started her own chocolate business. She makes the best candy! The big room attached to the kitchen is where she

8

does all her baking. It always smells good in there.

There are lots of pets at the big house too. David Michael has a Bernese mountain dog puppy named Shannon. We also have a black kitten, Pumpkin. Andrew has a goldfish he calls Goldfishie. My goldfish is named Crystal Light the Second. David Michael takes care of our fish when Andrew and I go to the little house.

Andrew and I switch houses every other month. He takes his hermit crab, Bob, and I take my rat, Emily, back and forth between the big house and the little house. But that's about all we need to take. You see, we have two of everything! Two mommies and two daddies, two houses, two cats, two dogs. One of each at the big house, and one of each at the little house. That's why I call my brother and me Andrew Two-Two and Karen Two-Two. (I thought up those names after Ms. Colman read a book to our class called *Jacob Two-Two Meets the Hooded Fang*.)

I have two sets of toys, two bicycles, two pairs of glasses (blue ones for reading and pink ones for the rest of the time), and best of all — two best friends!

Hannie and Nancy and I call ourselves the Three Musketeers because we do everything together. Hannie lives near the big house and Nancy lives next door to the little house. No matter which house I am in, I am near a Musketeer!

I could not wait to tell my friends and my whole family all about my ice skating lessons.

Lesson One

"**K**aren, let's get going!" Seth called. It was Saturday afternoon and I was almost ready for my first skating lesson.

I put an extra pair of socks in my skate bag and raced downstairs. I could not wait to get to the rink.

The Stoneybrook Ice Arena is near my little house. From the outside it looks like a huge white bubble. Andrew said it looks like a spaceship. Seth and Andrew came inside with me to help me find my class. A man behind a desk said I should put on my skates. My teacher would gather my class in a minute. I told Seth I would be okay by myself. So he and Andrew left the rink. I waved good-bye. I was ready to start my lessons.

Lots of students were in the arena already. But I did not know any of them. I looked around. To the left, I saw a large snack bar with tables and chairs. A few kids were laughing and talking. They looked as if they were having fun. I wished that Hannie and Nancy were taking lessons with me. Then the Three Musketeers would be sitting at the snack bar drinking hot chocolate. But my friends were not here. Several benches surrounded the oval rink, and lots of kids were lacing up their skates. I sat down on a bench by myself and tried to look like a real skater. I decided to put on my skates with the new neon-pink blade guards.

"Karen?"

I looked up and saw Ian Johnson. He is in Ms. Colman's class. Boy, I was happy to see him! I was so glad to have a friend at the arena with me.

"Are you taking skating lessons here too?" I asked Ian.

Ian looked around. He leaned in close to me and whispered, "Yes." Then he looked over his shoulder.

I was about to ask Ian why he was acting as if he were a spy on a secret mission when a woman with a clipboard in her hand walked over to us.

"Hello, I am Mrs. Harris," she said. "Welcome to the Stoneybrook Ice Arena. What are your names?"

Ian and I gave our names to Mrs. Harris, and she looked for them on her clipboard. She smiled and said, "Well, you are both in my class. Please stand by the entrance to the ice over there." I could see a few other kids already standing where she was pointing.

I slipped on my guards. Ian and I walked to the rink.

Mrs. Harris welcomed everyone. Including Ian and me, there were six kids in our group.

"This is the blade of your skate, and this is the toe pick." Mrs. Harris pointed to her skate.

I rolled my eyes at Ian. Well, of course we knew that.

Mrs. Harris told us that the first part of the lesson was called the warm-up skate. "Skaters need to get used to the ice by skating a few laps," she said. "Whenever you arrive at the rink, you should get on the ice and warm up." Then she told us that at the end of the lesson, we would have a free skate to practice what we had learned.

Next Mrs. Harris asked us all to get on the ice. Our class was in the far right corner of the rink. Mrs. Harris explained that she was going to show us the proper way to fall. "Every skater falls," she said. "It is important to learn the right way to fall, so you don't hurt yourself."

14

"This is baby stuff," I whispered to Ian as we skated to our section of the ice.

I noticed two girls from our class giggling and holding on to the side of the rink. They were already falling. And I did not think it was the right way. Ian and I seemed to be ahead of the rest of our class.

I wanted to spin like the skaters in the brochure. I was ready to twirl on the ice and make perfect jumps in the air. I did not want to learn how to fall down.

Maybe I was in the wrong class.

4

Keeping a Secret

"Very good, class," Mrs. Harris said. (She looked at Ian and me when she said it.)

The class was almost over. I liked the idea of the free skate at the end of our lesson. Then we did not have to stay with our class and we could skate around the whole rink.

Ian and I skated together. Ian was still acting strangely. He kept looking around. When we started our second lap around the rink, I finally asked him what was the matter.

"I am just checking to see if I know anyone here," Ian said. "I don't want anyone at school to know that I'm taking skating lessons." Ian turned and looked at me. "Karen, do you promise not to tell anyone about this? Especially no one in our class?"

"Why?" I asked. I could not wait to tell the kids in our class about our skating lessons.

"I do not want anyone to make fun of me," Ian whispered. He looked worried. "Not many boys take skating lessons."

"I promise," I said.

As we glided around the corner, I realized that Ian was right. There were not many boys at the rink. I also noticed that Ian was a very good skater. He was almost as good as me.

"Ian," I said, "lots of boys skate. Some even win gold medals. Maybe you could win one too!"

Ian smiled. I smiled back at him. "You are a good skater," I told him.

"Thanks, Karen," Ian said. "You are too."

"I cannot wait until we learn how to do

spins and jumps. I think that we are the best skaters in our class," I said. "Did you see those two girls, Kelly and Alyse?"

Ian laughed. "Yeah, they did not let go of the railing during the whole class!"

"We should be in a more advanced class," I said. "I want to do things like that girl over there." I pointed to an area behind red cones at the far end of the rink.

Ian told me that area was reserved for Coach Brown's students. Coach Brown was famous for coaching Olympic champions. He even coached a gold medalist named Michael Phaneuf. We both stopped and watched his student, a girl with a brown ponytail, spin like a top.

"Wow, she is really good," I said. I had only seen spins like that on television. And she did the spin perfectly.

"That is Jillian Earhart," Ian said. "Coach Brown is training her here. My cousin Jessica told me. She took lessons here last year."

Ian and I stopped skating and hung out

on the side of the rink to watch Jillian skate. Coach Brown fixed her arms as she came out of her spin and motioned for her to do the move again.

"Some people think Jillian is going to the next Olympics," Ian added.

I could not believe it. Jillian was a real Olympic skater!

"Cool," I said. I wanted to learn to skate just like her.

"She is thirteen years old and she could win the gold," Ian said.

I was so happy. I was in the same rink as an Olympic hopeful.

And if my lessons got any better, maybe someday I would be one too!

Hot-Chocolate Break

"It is time to go!" Andrew called upstairs to me.

I was rushing to get ready for skating class after school on Wednesday. Our nanny, Merry, was waiting for me. She had to take Andrew to a birthday party across town, so I had to go to the rink a little early. I did not mind. I would get to see Jillian skate again. If I watched her closely, maybe I could learn a thing or two.

In the car, Andrew talked about his friend's party at the Swinging Monkey's

Gym. But all I could think about was skating. When we reached the arena, Merry turned to me in the backseat. "We will see you later, Karen," she said. "Have fun!"

I grabbed my skating bag and hopped out of the car. " 'Bye!" I called. "Have fun at the party, Andrew."

Inside the arena, students were already on the ice warming up. From the benches I could see Jillian and Coach Brown. Today Jillian was wearing black stretch pants and a pink fuzzy sweater. I love fuzzy pink sweaters. I watched Jillian land two double axels. Her jumps were perfect. I wished that I could do that.

I laced up my skates and stepped out onto the ice. As I skated around the rink, I saw Kelly and Alyse, still holding on to the wall.

"Hi, Karen," Kelly said.

"Hi," I replied.

"She is so great," Alyse said, pointing at Jillian.

The three of us watched as Jillian landed

two more double axels. "I wish that I could skate like her," Kelly said.

"I wish that I could meet her," Alyse added. "She is going to be a star at the Olympics."

"Great job, Jillian," Coach Brown said. "Let's take a quick break and we will try out the new combination."

Jillian skated to the wall and stepped off the ice. Suddenly I had a gigundoly great idea! I looked up at the large clock in the center of the rink. I had lots of time before my lesson started. Perfect!

I said good-bye to Kelly and Alyse and skated off the ice. Inside my bag, I found some money. I slipped my skating guards on my blades and headed to the snack counter. Across the rink, I watched Jillian stretch and sit down on a bench. My plan was going to work just fine.

I ordered two cups of hot chocolate and walked around the rink to where Jillian was sitting.

"Hi," I said. "My name is Karen Brewer. Would you like some hot chocolate?"

Jillian looked surprised to see me standing there with hot chocolate. I do not think many people went to that side of the rink. Or maybe she was not used to getting treats from her fans.

"Thank you," Jillian said. She had a great smile.

"You are really good. I am a huge fan of yours," I said.

"Thank you. Are you taking lessons here?"

I told her that I was in Mrs. Harris's class.

"Mrs. Harris was my first teacher here at the rink." Jillian said. "She is really nice and she is a very good teacher."

"Really? I think the class is too easy."

Jillian smiled. "You will learn the basics. That is important for all skaters."

"When did you start skating?" I asked.

"When I was seven."

"I am seven!" I said, smiling. We had so much in common already.

Jillian took a sip of her hot chocolate. She told me that she had been training with Coach Brown for the last four years. "Once he showed me how to do my patchwork, I knew I wanted to be a skater."

"What is patchwork?" I asked.

"It is all the required moves that a skater must do for competitions," she explained. "You know, like a figure eight."

I was not sure what Jillian meant, so she put down her cup and stepped onto the ice. On one foot she traced out the bottom loop of an eight. Then she switched feet and looped the top. She was very graceful.

"That is so cool!" I said.

"That is what I thought when Coach Brown did it too," Jillian said as she skated back to the wall. "After he showed me all those moves, I knew that I wanted to be a skater."

Well, I already knew that. And I was on my way to learning how to be a perfect one!

6

Skating Star

During dinner that night I told my little-house family all about Jillian. I told them about the cups of hot chocolate and the perfect figure eight. I could not stop talking about meeting her.

"She must have very little free time," Seth said. "It is hard to compete in skating."

"She must really love the sport," Mommy added.

"I love skating too," I said. When I finished my meal, I was supposed to do my homework. But I was too excited. I wanted to call the Musketeers and tell them that I met the star skater at the ice arena.

No one was home at Hannie's house, so I called Nancy next. Nancy clicked over from another call. She was on the other line — with Ian.

I almost said, "Tell Ian that I spoke to Jillian!" But I stopped myself. That would give Ian's secret away. Nancy would know that he was taking skating lessons with me. And I had promised not to tell.

"Karen, can I call you back?" Nancy said. "Ian and I are working on some homework."

"Sure," I said. "Tell Ian that I said hi." I figured that was safe. I, Karen Brewer, can keep an important secret.

Then I decided to call my big sister, Kristy. I figured she would be very impressed that I had a new friend who was a skating star. As it turned out, Kristy knew Jillian! They used to be in the same class at Stoneybrook Elementary School.

"I haven't seen Jillian in a long time," Kristy said. "She left school to train full-time, and now she has tutors for her school-work."

"Jillian had my teacher when she was my age. I want to be just like her," I told Kristy.

"Karen," Kristy said, "Jillian has had to make a lot of sacrifices. That means she had to give up things to get where she is now. She works very hard at her skating. She does not have a lot of time to hang out with her friends. It is a tough life."

"I am her friend," I said. "She had time to hang out with me today." I was not sure what Kristy meant about sacrifices. Did she mean missing school? That did not seem so bad for someone who had a chance to win at the Olympics. Jillian loved being a skating star. She did not mention giving up things to me.

"I think that it is nice that you are friends

with Jillian, Karen," Kristy said. "She probably would appreciate having a friend like
you."

When I hung up the phone, I smiled. I
was proud and happy. Jillian Earhart, the
skating star, was my friend.

7

My New Friend

During Friday's warm-up skate, I skated by the red cones and waved to Jillian. She was talking to Coach Brown, so I did not think she saw me. He was moving her arms in different directions and making her do the same move again and again.

Then Mrs. Harris called our class together in the blue-cone area. She showed us how to do forward crossovers. Ian and I knew how to do those already. We had been doing them all week. So while Mrs. Harris was helping the other kids in the class, Ian and I practiced skating backward.

I told Ian about meeting Jillian. "She is so nice. And she had Mrs. Harris as a teacher, just like us," I said.

Ian thought that was cool. He said that he had seen Jillian on television the month before, and she had won a big competition. "She was much, much better than everybody else," he added. "But I wish someone like Michael Phaneuf trained here."

I wondered if Ian said that because he would rather meet a boy skater.

"Nice skating, Karen and Ian!" Mrs. Harris called to us.

We smiled. But we were still wondering when Mrs. Harris would tell us that we could move up to another class.

I tried to help Kelly and Alyse with their crossovers, but it was hard to show them when they would not let go of the wall.

Soon it was time for the free skate. Ian was leaving early to go to his grandmother's house. I was sorry that he had to leave. But I was happy that I could stay and practice. I could watch Jillian too. I did not expect to talk to her again, but I knew I could learn by copying what she did on the ice.

I skated near the red cones and watched out of the corner of my eye. Coach Brown was not there anymore, but Jillian was practicing her sit spins. She waved at me when she finished one.

"Hi, Karen!" she said.

"Hi, Jillian!" I called back proudly. I wished Ian were there to see this.

Jillian skated over to the red cone where I was standing. I could not believe it. She wanted to talk to me again.

"How was your lesson?" Jillian asked.

I told her about the crossovers. I even told her that Mrs. Harris's class was easy, because I knew how to do the moves already.

"Well, maybe I can teach you something trickier. Do you know how to do a waltz jump?" Jillian said.

I did not know. So Jillian showed me. She leaped up and turned gracefully. Jillian showed me how to bend my knees going into the jump and to hold my arms. "And remember to keep your head up," she added.

As we skated in the red-cone area, I felt very special. Especially when I looked up and saw Kelly and Alyse watching.

I did another waltz jump and Jillian clapped. She was a great teacher.

"Your class will probably learn this in a few weeks," Jillian said. "I loved doing these when I was your age."

Jillian was teaching me some of her favorite moves!

The free skate was almost over. I could not believe how much time Jillian had spent with me. Maybe Kristy was right and Jillian really needed a friend. She probably did not see many kids. I could be her friend. After all, I was going to be a star skater just like her.

8

Gold Medal Dreams

The next day was Saturday, and I was back at the rink.

I saw Ian on the benches lacing up his skates. I sat down next to him to say that Jillian had showed me how to do a waltz jump. "I will show you how to do it during the free skate," I said. I did not want him to feel left out.

"The rest of the kids in our class will not learn how to do the jump for a few weeks," I said. "They are not as advanced as we are."

When the free skate started, I did the waltz jump for Ian. Then I tried to be a good teacher like Jillian. But Ian got a little mad when I told him to keep his head up.

"You don't have to be so bossy, Karen," he said. "I am just going to practice my backward crossovers."

Well, boo and bullfrogs. I was only trying to help. Maybe Ian did not want to learn from a girl skater. I skated the length of the rink and passed the red-cone area. I was careful to make all my crossovers very clean in case Jillian was watching.

"Hi, Karen!" Jillian said as she waved to me. "Come here. I would like you to meet somebody very special."

I was going inside the red-cone area again! I skated to where Jillian and her coach were standing.

"Jeremy, this is Karen Brewer, the girl I was telling you about," Jillian said.

Coach Brown was tall and had a nice, friendly smile. He shook my hand and then put his hand on my shoulder.

"Jillian says that you are a great skater."

An Olympic coach had heard that I was a great skater! I could not say anything (which is not at all like me). All I could do was smile.

"Karen is in Mrs. Harris's class, just like I was when I was little," Jillian said.

Coach Brown smiled again. "How are the lessons going, Karen?" he asked.

"Oh, I love skating," I replied, and smiled at Jillian. "Jillian showed me how to do a waltz jump. Most of the kids in my class are not ready to learn how to do that yet."

Coach Brown smiled at Jillian. "Karen, have you ever been to a skating competition?"

"No," I said.

"Jillian has a competition this Friday night. Would you like to come see her perform?"

Goody, goody, goody! "Oh, yes!" I said.

Jillian laughed, and so did Coach Brown.

"I will get you some backstage passes," Coach Brown said.

"I will have to ask my mommy," I said. "But I'm sure that it will be okay with her."

"Just have your mother call me here at the rink and we will set everything up." Coach Brown was so nice. I bet he was this nice to Jillian all the time. Jillian was a lucky skater to have such a great coach!

I thanked Coach Brown and Jillian and left the red-cone area. I did another few turns on the rink, making perfect crossovers. I hoped Coach Brown was watching. I did not need Mrs. Harris anymore. She was a teacher for little kids. An Olympic hopeful needed a real coach, like Jeremy Brown.

Now that I was friends with Jillian and her coach, I could see my whole skating career coming together. I would train with Coach Brown and prepare for big competitions just like the one I was about to see. I would skate a perfect routine at the Olympics. I would have a spangly outfit with lots of sequins. Everyone would comment on how great I looked out on the rink. When my perfect routine was over, the sold-out crowd would jump to their feet, applaud very loudly, and shout my name. Then I would stand on the platform with loads of flowers as the National Anthem played throughout the large arena. The judge would walk toward me and I would bend my head for her to award me with a gold medal.

I would wave to my family and all my friends. I would be Karen Brewer, gold-medal skating star!

9

A Big Break

All day Wednesday I waited for school to be over. In the afternoon, Nancy, Hannie, Natalie, Ian, Chris, and I worked on our Abraham Lincoln poster for Presidents' Day. It was a life-size picture. Ms. Colman was going to hang it in the classroom. I was busy coloring in Lincoln's hat, but I kept looking at the clock above the door. I love school, but I wanted to get to the rink to tell Jillian that I was allowed to go to her competition! Even Ms. Colman asked me why I was so eager for the final bell to ring. (She knows that I usually love school.)

I saw Jillian as soon as I entered the arena. A very pretty woman was showing her different hand motions. I waved, but Jillian did not see me. I would have to tell her about the competition later.

As Ian and I were getting ready to step on the ice, Mrs. Harris sat down next to us.

"Hi, you two," she said. "I want to talk to you about something."

I could not believe it. Was Mrs. Harris going to ask me if I wanted to work with Coach Brown? Did she have the same Olympic dream for me too?

"A week from Saturday, we are having the Festival on Ice here at the arena," she said. "The festival is where the best skaters from all age levels perform. I would love it if you both would skate in the show."

Ian and I looked at each other. We grinned. I did not know what Ian was thinking. But I was thinking this could be my big break!

Finally Mrs. Harris was noticing my talent (and Ian's).

"You will be representing our class at the show," she added.

"Will we get to wear fancy costumes?" I asked.

"Of course," Mrs. Harris said with a smile.

"How many other kids are skating?" Ian asked.

"Oh, let me see. Probably about twenty. This is our biggest festival yet."

"What music will I skate to?" Ian asked.

"Well, I was hoping that you and Karen would skate as a pair," Mrs. Harris said. "We have not chosen the music yet, though."

I had not thought about skating with a partner. I looked at Ian. He did not seem very happy about that idea.

Mrs. Harris smiled. "I think that you and Karen will make an excellent skating pair. But it will take lots of hard work to prepare for the show. You will have to practice many hours."

I knew that skating was hard work. I was

ready for it. After all, this could be my big chance. Maybe Mrs. Harris was doing this as a test for us before we could move into an advanced class. I was ready to pass with flying colors.

But Ian shrugged his shoulders. He was not worried about the hard work, it turned out. He was worried about skating with me. "Um, do we have to hold hands while we skate?"

Well, for goodness' sake!

Mrs. Harris smiled and put her hand on Ian's shoulder. "Not the whole time, but you will have to hold Karen's hand some of the time." She looked at Ian and then at me. "But you are good friends, right?"

I watched Ian. I hoped he would nod yes. I really wanted to skate in the Festival on Ice.

"It will be fun, Ian," I said.

Ian slowly nodded. He agreed. It was all set. Ian and I were going to skate in the Festival on Ice!

During the free skate I told Jillian my

news. I told her about the festival and that I could go to her competition.

"Great, Karen!" she said. "I will see you Friday night at the competition."

I skated away feeling very happy. I was finally on my way to becoming the next Jillian Earhart!

10

Skating Show

On Friday after school Mommy took me to the florist to get a bouquet of flowers for Jillian. We also got her a teddy bear with a T-shirt that said #1. I could not wait to go to my first real skating competition.

Seth drove Mommy, Andrew, and me to Lawrenceville Rink, where the competition was being held. There were lots of cars in the parking lot. This was a big event.

Coach Brown had gotten us great seats. I was so close to the ice! I loved seeing all the lights and hearing the music play. Every seat was taken. The crowd was very excited and so was I.

I looked at the program of skaters. Lots of boys were skating. (I would be sure to tell Ian that the next day.) But the first skater was a girl named Caroline Jones. She did all her jumps perfectly and the crowd roared with applause. I opened the program again and counted the skaters. There were three more before Jillian's turn.

When Jillian skated out to the center of the rink, I could hardly breathe! Jillian looked glamorous. She was wearing a lavender dress, and her hair was tied with purple flowers. A bright-blue spotlight focused on her. (I decided that I would want that for the beginning of my skating performance too.) The crowd cheered, and then her music began. It was the "Dance of the Sugar Plum Fairy" from *The Nutcracker*.

"She is perfect," I said to Mommy as Jillian started to skate. She landed two double toe loops in a row. Everyone cheered.

The music sped up and Jillian did her first

triple axel jump. I had seen her do these in practice. She was really good at jumps. She twirled up in the air and rotated around three times. But on her landing, her foot wobbled and she fell.

The crowd all sighed, "Ooh!"

Poor Jillian. I leaned forward in my seat to see what would happen next. She got up right away and continued with her program. She even had a huge smile on her face. I was sure the judges would give her credit for getting up after a fall. After all, Jillian had the courage to keep going with her program. As the final chord of the music played, Jillian was back in the center of the rink with her hands high up over her head. She smiled and waved at the crowd. Then she skated to the side of the rink, hugged Coach Brown, and disappeared. Mommy pointed to the large board in the center of the rink, where the judges' scores would appear.

I watched the board. I squeezed Jillian's bear and crossed my fingers for good luck.

"Oh, please. Oh, please," I said over and over, hoping for Jillian's scores to be good.

The bright-red numbers of the first score made the crowd boo. It was a low score. And so was the next one. And the next one. I could not believe it. Jillian finished the competition in fifth place.

Flowers and Teddy Bears

The lights dimmed in the large arena for the award ceremony. I could not believe that Jillian was not the girl on the center platform receiving flowers from the judge. Caroline Jones, the first skater, was the winner. She waved and smiled at the crowd.

When the ceremony was over, Mommy and Seth said that we should go backstage to give Jillian her gifts. I was excited about going behind the scenes. I thought I would find lots of people with cameras and microphones. Maybe a television reporter would want to ask me a few questions, since I was a friend of Jillian's.

When we walked backstage, I looked for Jillian. But I did not see her anywhere. Finally Mommy asked someone where we could find her, and we headed for a little room in the back.

Jillian was sitting on a bench with an ice pack on her ankle. She was wearing her warm-up sweats. There were no reporters or cameras around her. She was just sitting quietly with Coach Brown. I thought that Jillian might be crying. If I fell during my program, I would cry. But Jillian did not look as though she had been crying.

"Hi, Jillian," I said. I handed her the flowers and the teddy bear. She smiled. (I think that she really liked the bear.) I introduced Mommy, Seth, and Andrew to Jillian and Coach Brown.

"You had a difficult program," Mommy said. "You are a terrific skater."

"Thank you," Jillian replied. She shifted her foot and winced a little. She must have hurt her foot during the routine.

"Is your ankle okay?" Andrew asked. He was staring at the large blue ice pack.

"It will be fine," Jillian said. "I just twisted it." Jillian looked up at Coach Brown and he gave her a hug. "This was not my best performance." She sighed.

"Jillian is a champion," Coach Brown said. "But sometimes even champions have bad days."

"I knew that my landing was not perfect. I felt it. But these things happen," Jillian explained.

I could not believe how brave Jillian was being. She was so calm, even though she had made such a big mistake.

"Jillian never gives up on her positive thinking. That is what makes her a star," Coach Brown said. "Every skater falls down sometimes. The true test of a champion is whether she gets up."

We all wished Jillian well and headed out

of the arena. I was a little disappointed. I had expected to see the television crews and groups of fans. The scene behind the competition was not what I thought it would be.

On the way home I looked out the window and thought about the Festival on Ice. I hoped that my own performance the next week would go better than Jillian's today. Mrs. Harris said that Ian and I had to practice. Well, I was going to practice every day! I did not want to fall in front of all those people. I was not sure I could pick myself up and keep skating. I was not sure I would want to do that either.

12

Hard Work

I was ready to start working on my routine for my performance in the Festival on Ice. I could take hard work. After all, I too was a star skater. And I did not want to make any big mistakes. I arrived at the rink and spotted Jillian right away. She was wearing a yellow wrap sweater and black leggings. In the center of the rink she did three perfect jumps. It was too bad they were so much better than the jump she had done in her competition. I guess her ankle was better.

I laced up my skates and glided to the red cone by the wall.

Jillian waved and skated toward me. I was a little nervous. What was I supposed to say? I did not know if she was upset about her performance.

"Hi, Karen!" Jillian called.

"Hi!" I said. I gave her one of my special big Karen Brewer smiles.

"So did Mrs. Harris show you the routine for Saturday?" she asked. We talked about the Festival on Ice. Jillian did not seem sad or different at all. I could not believe it.

"It is really cool when you get your first skating routine," Jillian said. Her eyes were wide with excitement as she told me about the first routine that Mrs. Harris had choreographed for her.

"I am so excited about my routine," I said.

"It's for you and your partner, Ian, right?" Jillian said.

"Right."

The warm-up skate was over and kids were starting to gather at the corners of the rink. I said good-bye to Jillian and stood with my class.

During the free skate Mrs. Harris told Ian and me that she wanted to show us our routine. Ian and I smiled at each other. We were both excited to see what moves Mrs. Harris was going to teach us. And what music we would use for our routine.

I watched Mrs. Harris as she skated around the back corner of the rink doing crossovers and the waltz jump. (I was so glad that Jillian had showed me how to do that already.)

After we practiced the jumps, Mrs. Harris told me to hold Ian's hands. I thought that Ian was going to make a face, but he was trying to be professional, just like me. We skated around the rink holding hands.

Once we learned the first part of the program, Mrs. Harris said she had a new move to show us. She told me to hold my leg straight out behind me. Ian was going to hold my hands and skate backward while I

58

stuck out my leg. "Extend your back leg and hold it up, Karen," Mrs. Harris said.

It was hard to keep my leg up.

"Concentrate!" Mrs. Harris kept saying. "Karen, keep your head up!" At the end of the free skate, Mrs. Harris wanted to talk about costumes. "Karen, what color would you like your costume to be?"

I took a moment to think about it. After all, this was important. I might be on television and in the newspapers. Mrs. Harris gave me a Look. I guess she wanted to order these costumes right away. "Pink," I said.

"Good choice," Mrs. Harris replied. "I bet that we could even put some sequins on it." She winked at me and I smiled at her. I could not wait to see my spangly new skating outfit.

"Um, what am I going to wear?" Ian said. I could tell he did not want to wear a pink sequined outfit. "How about one of those hockey jerseys?"

Mrs. Harris frowned. "Ian, we will get

you a nice, simple blue shirt and pants. What do you think of that?"

Ian seemed relieved. I think his favorite color is blue.

By the time I took off my skates, my legs were feeling shaky. I was tired and a bit sore. The routine was hard work.

My big break was going to be harder than I had thought.

13

Practice Makes Perfect

At school on Monday morning I told Ms. Colman about my new skating outfit. "That sounds wonderful," she said. She gave me a big smile and patted my shoulder. I hoped that she would come see me skate at the show.

Nancy and Hannie were talking about a new movie, *The Secrets of the Unicorns.* They were talking with Natalie about the beautiful white unicorn.

"When did you see the movie?" I asked. I

wondered why they had not asked me to go with them.

"We all saw it this weekend," Natalie said.

When Natalie left, Nancy turned to me. "What is wrong, Karen?" she asked.

"Well, I thought the Three Musketeers always went to the movies together," I replied.

"We wanted you to come, Karen," Hannie said. "But my mom could only take us on Saturday afternoon. And you were at your skating lesson."

I looked at Hannie and Nancy. I *had* been at my lesson on Saturday. But I was still sad that I hadn't gone with my best friends to the movies. Maybe this was what Kristy meant about sacrifices and star skaters.

"I am going to be the star at the Festival on Ice in two weeks," I blurted out. "I am going to have a fancy costume and everything."

"That is great!" Nancy said.

"Can we come and watch?" Hannie asked.

I was so happy that my friends wanted to see me skate. And Musketeers do not stay mad long. So I said yes and forgot about being mad. But that is not all I forgot about. I had also forgotten that Ian did not want people to know he was taking skating lessons.

Nancy invited Hannie and me to her house after school. But I could not go. I had to go to an extra skating practice. I was disappointed that I could not be with my friends. I told them that a real skating star has to be at the rink a lot.

During practice Ian kept skating too fast. He was not listening to the music. But Mrs. Harris was only correcting me!

"Karen, watch your footing."

"Karen, arch your back."

"Karen, practice makes perfect. One more time."

Well, boo and bullfrogs. What about Ian?

"Good work, Ian," Mrs. Harris said.

64

She must have forgotten that I was her new star skater.

"Don't worry, you will have more practice time before the festival," Mrs. Harris said. "Practice will make all the difference."

I know, I thought. *Practice makes perfect.* But I did not need more practice. Ian needed to slow down. And Mrs. Harris was forgetting that I, Karen Brewer, was the next Jillian Earhart.

When Seth arrived to pick me up, Mrs. Harris asked him if I would be able to come to another extra practice the next day.

At this rate I would never see my friends. But my part of the show was sure to be perfect.

14

Keep Trying

I was happy to see Jillian at the rink on Tuesday afternoon. I wanted to talk to her about my costume. Maybe she would tell me about her costume for her first performance. I wondered if it was as beautiful as mine.

But Jillian did not want to talk about costumes. She wanted to know about my routine, and she could not wait to help me with it. She said that she would take Ian's role and that I could practice my part. We were about to start when Mrs. Harris skated over to us.

"Ian is going to be about fifteen minutes late today, Karen," she said. "But I am glad that you are using this time to practice." She smiled at Jillian. "And you have a great coach helping you."

"Yes," I said, smiling up at Jillian.

"When you are finished, you can come by the office," Mrs. Harris said. "I received the costumes for Saturday. You should try yours on."

Oh, goody! I wanted to try it on right away.

"Come on, Karen," Jillian said. "Show me the rest of your combination."

I wanted to try on my new outfit. But I also wanted to be with Jillian. I did the leg extension holding Jillian's hands.

"Karen, you are not concentrating," Jillian said.

"Maybe we could get some hot chocolate and I could try on my outfit?" I said.

"I thought you wanted to practice. You know what Mrs. Harris says —"

"Practice makes perfect!" we exclaimed, and laughed.

"Maybe you could show me how to do a figure eight again," I said. "I think that will help me to focus."

Jillian smiled at me. "How about we do your routine one more time, and then I'll show you the figure eight?"

That sounded like a good plan to me. (Maybe we could get hot chocolate afterwards.) I skated the routine with Jillian, counting out all the moves (we did not have the music on). I could not wait to get it over with. When we finally finished, I watched Jillian trace out two perfect loops to form a beautiful number eight on the ice.

I pushed off on one foot just like Jillian had done, but I did not get halfway around the first loop! I tried again, but it was too hard.

"Don't get frustrated, Karen," Jillian said. "It takes —"

"I know, it takes *practice*." I sighed.

"Keep trying, you'll get it," Jillian said.

Just then I saw Ian skating around the

rink. I was glad that he had arrived. I did not think that I was going to skate a perfect eight today. Now that Ian had arrived, I could at least go see my pink spangly skating outfit.

15

Silent Partner

At school the next morning, Hannie and Nancy were waiting for me on the playground.

"Guess what, Karen?" Nancy said. She was grinning and jumping up and down. "We have a big surprise for you!"

"What?" I asked. I love surprises.

"We told everyone in Ms. Colman's class about your skating show!" Nancy said.

"And everyone is coming to see you, Karen Brewer, star skater!" Hannie added.

"Everyone?" I said. Oh, no! Then everyone would find out about Ian's lessons. I had broken my promise to Ian.

"Karen, what is the matter?" Hannie asked. "We thought you would be happy."

I did not have a chance to answer because the bell rang and we went inside to Ms. Colman's classroom. I looked around at my friends in the room. Then I spotted Ian. He was glaring at me.

"I hear everyone is going to see you skate in *your* skating show this weekend," he whispered.

"Ian, I am sorry. I did not mean for the whole class to find out," I whispered back.

Ian just stared at me. His stare said everything. I knew that I had let him down. I had broken my promise. Sort of.

Ms. Colman asked us to take our seats. I felt awful. I wanted to talk to Ian. All day long I tried to talk to him. And every time I did he would turn away. Even during gym, when we were on the same team, he would not speak to me.

I thought that Ian and I could at least talk

at skating practice. But still he would not even look at me. Mrs. Harris said that we should skate without music so we could count out the routine. She asked Ian to start to count. Then we would do our moves at the same time. When we got on the ice, he would not say a word. Not even one, two, three.

"Ian, we have to count together," I said. "I really am sorry."

Ian looked right past me. He started to do the waltz jump before I did. He turned before I turned. I tried to catch up to him, but my footing was off and I fell twice.

"Talk to each other," Mrs. Harris called from the side. "You need to count together."

I was getting angry at Ian. How was I supposed to skate with a silent partner? I had told him I was sorry. And I could not help it if Hannie and Nancy had told everyone about the Festival on Ice.

I tripped over Ian's skate as we were doing a backward crossover.

"Karen, concentrate!" Mrs. Harris called.

I was tired of skating, tired of falling, and, most of all, tired of my silent partner. I missed my friends. I missed my life. I skated over to the wall and hopped off the ice.

I turned to Ian and said, "I quit!"

Good Advice

When I turned around, I saw Jillian standing there. She had heard what I said. I started to cry. Ian was mad at me already. I did not want Jillian to be mad at me too.

Jillian put her arm around me. "Want some hot chocolate?" she asked.

I snuffled a little and looked at Jillian. She did not look mad. I nodded and followed her to the snack bar.

"You know, Karen," Jillian said, "skating is a lot of fun, but it is lots of hard work."

Boy, I was starting to see that! I told Jillian

about Ian's secret and how I missed my friends.

"I used to have more time to be with my friends," I said. Then I told Jillian about missing *The Secrets of the Unicorns*. "If I had gone to the movies with my friends, I would not have felt left out. And I might not have invited them to the Festival on Ice. And they would not have told everyone in our class about it." I took a deep breath. "Then Ian would not be mad at me for not keeping his secret.

Jillian listened carefully. She told me that I should remember how much I loved skating. "You have to focus on why you are here," she said. She sounded a lot like Coach Brown or Mrs. Harris. "Do not worry so much about what your friends think." I started to feel better. I blew my nose and settled into my chair to listen to Jillian. She was right. I had to think about my skating. "When you are skating, do you feel your best? Do you love the feeling of landing a jump or completing a routine?" I watched

Jillian as she talked about skating. Her eyes were wide and happy. Jillian did not just sound like a grown-up anymore. She sounded like a skater who loved to skate. I did not think about skating like that. I had thought I was the next Jillian Earhart. But I was not very much like her at all. Jillian was different.

"I am tired of skating all the time," I said.

Jillian laughed. "It has only been a couple of weeks, Karen!"

I laughed too. Jillian was being so nice to me. How could I quit?

"Will you skate in the show, Karen?" Jillian asked. "I am sure that you and Ian will work things out. After all, you are partners. And more important, you are friends."

I nodded. I could not let Jillian down. I agreed to be in the Festival on Ice. I would just have to talk to my friends and Ian.

17

The Secret

On Thursday morning before the bell rang for school, I found Nancy and Hannie. I took them to a corner of the playground so we could talk in private.

"This is a Three Musketeers secret," I said. "Promise not to tell anyone?"

My two best friends agreed. I leaned over and whispered that Ian Johnson was my skating partner in the show. I explained that he was embarrassed about skating and did not want the whole class to know.

"Why did he not want anyone to know?" Nancy asked.

"Why would he want to keep skating a secret?" Hannie said. "I bet he is a great skater."

"He is a great skater," I replied. But then I told them how I had broken Ian's promise.

"We are sorry, Karen," Nancy said.

"Ian must really be mad," Hannie added.

I could tell that my friends felt bad.

The bell rang then, and all the kids went inside to start the day.

Natalie was standing by my desk. She looked at us Musketeers. "What is wrong? You look so sad." We must have been thinking about Ian's problem.

"You have to promise not to tell anyone, Natalie," I said.

Natalie traced an X across her chest. "I promise," she said.

I told Natalie about Ian's skating lessons and that the whole class would soon find out about them. "Remember, Natalie," I said. "Do not tell anyone."

At lunchtime, I saw Natalie, Hannie, and Nancy talking to Ricky and Chris. I hoped that they were not telling them Ian's secret.

At recess, I found out that everyone in Ms. Colman's class knew about Ian. When Ian walked past me on the playground, I could tell that he knew everyone knew too.

I stomped over to Hannie and Nancy. "How could you tell everyone Ian's secret? I asked you not to tell anyone!"

"We did not tell anyone," Nancy said.

"Natalie told everyone," Hannie said. "And you were the one who told her."

Oh! I was so mad! I watched Natalie playing hopscotch across the playground. How could she have done that?

Ian was standing by the swing set. I thought that I would try to talk to him again. Now I had to apologize for Natalie's big mouth too. But before I could talk to Ian, Ricky ran to him. "Hey, Ian, can you skate backward?"

"How fast can you skate around the rink?" Chris asked.

"And can you do those jumps?" Bobby added.

I watched Ian answer our friends' questions. Suddenly he did not seem to mind taking skating lessons anymore.

"That is so cool that you and Karen are going to skate at the Stoneybrook Ice Arena," Chris said. "That place is awesome!"

"Yeah, the Penguins skate there. I saw a game last week," Bobby said. "The place is huge!"

"And I saw a skating competition on television that was there," Hannie said. "You and Karen are going to be like real skating stars on Saturday."

Ian looked at me and smiled. I did not think that he was mad at me anymore. And then he told our friends that he hoped that they would all come to see us skate on Saturday.

"We are going to practice together after school today, right, Karen?" Ian asked.

I was glad that we were friends again. I smiled at him. "Yes," I said. But I felt a little funny. I was nervous about the big show.

As we walked back into our classroom, I gave my two best friends a quick hug. "I am sorry that I said you blabbed a secret."

I realized then how much I missed my friends. I was really glad that I was a Musketeer. I was also glad that soon skating would be over so I could spend more time with them. Kristy was right. A star skater has to make sacrifices. I did not want to make any more sacrifices! I did not want to give up anything. Being a star skater was a lot more work than I thought it would be.

18

A Couple of Stars

"Happy Valentine's Day!" Andrew said to me. He was sitting at the kitchen table eating his breakfast. Mommy had made red frosted cupcakes for both my class and Andrew's. I was excited about bringing them into school. And I could not wait to get valentine cards! I had decorated a shoe box as my mailbox.

School was fun. We had a party and read our valentines. Ian gave me one that said:

To my favorite skating partner.
Your friend,
Ian

I gave him one too. I wrote:

TO A #1 SKATING STAR!
YOUR FRIEND,
KAREN

Our show was to take place the very next day. At the rink red-and-pink hearts and balloons were everywhere. There was even a red spotlight on the rink!

Mrs. Harris started our music, and Ian and I began our routine. We counted together and did everything perfectly.

"Well done!" Mrs. Harris said. "I think you are ready for the show tomorrow night."

"I think we are too," Ian said. We skated to the side of the rink and stepped off the ice. We were about to take off our skates when Jillian walked into the arena. She was wearing a red sweater. And she was walking with a boy! Maybe he was Jillian's valentine. He was very cute.

"Hi, Karen! Hi, Ian!" Jillian said. She brought the boy to where we were sitting.

Ian's face burst into a huge grin. "You're Roman Legedza!"

Jillian and Roman laughed. "Yes, that is right," the boy said. "I am Roman Legedza."

Jillian introduced us to Roman.

"Wow," Ian said. "You are, like, the best male skater in the whole world!"

"Thank you," Roman said. "That is a huge compliment."

Jillian told us that Roman won the gold medal in the last Olympics and that he was training in a nearby town. She said they had been friends for a long time.

"Are you skating in tomorrow's show?" Roman asked.

"Yes," Ian and I said together.

"Could I see you do one of those flips that

you did last month at the Nationals?" Ian asked Roman.

Roman smiled. "Sure, but why don't you show me one of your moves first?"

Roman and Ian went out on the ice. I turned to Jillian. I was not sure what to say to her. How could I tell her that I had decided not to be a star skater like she was? I bet she noticed that I did not recognize Roman Legedza. I wondered if Jillian knew that I wanted to quit skating. I still wanted to be her friend. Would she be mad at me?

19

Push and Glide

I was playing with the strap on my skate bag as I watched Ian and Roman skate. I was trying hard not to look at Jillian. I did not want to tell her that I was finished with skating lessons.

"Karen," Jillian said. "You know, you can love the sport of skating without making it your career. It is hard work and it is not for everyone."

I wondered how she had known just what to say. I finally looked up at her. "I really wanted to be just like you," I said. "But I do not think that I can. I did not realize how hard it was going to be."

Jillian smiled and gave me a hug. "You are a great skater, Karen. And tomorrow you and Ian will have a chance to perform in front of lots of people."

"I know. But I did not want to disappoint you."

"You have not disappointed me. You helped me to remember how much I love skating and how much I love this sport." Jillian smiled at me. "And you also made me realize how lucky I am. I have a wonderful coach and very good friends . . . like you."

"I did all that?" I said.

Jillian laughed. "Yes, silly. You did."

I was glad that Jillian was not mad at me. But there was one more thing that I needed to ask her.

"Jillian, I know that I will never be as good as you. But could you just help me to make one real figure eight?"

"Sure," Jillian said. She laced up her skates, and we stepped onto the ice. The ice had just been cleaned, so there were no blade marks. The surface was smooth and clear. Perfect for making eights, Jillian told me.

I got into position. I tried to remember everything Jillian had done.

"Push and glide," she coached. I glided around and made a wobbly loop. I switched my foot at the top and pushed off to form the bottom loop of the eight.

"Great job!" Jillian said. I looked down at the ice. There on the shiny surface was an eight! I had made a figure eight!

I gave Jillian a hug. "Thank you!" I said.

"You did it all yourself," Jillian said. "Karen Brewer, you are a star!"

20

Festival on Ice

When I woke up on Saturday, I was excited. The ice show was that night. I called the big house to make sure that everyone there was coming to see my show. Elizabeth answered the phone and said that the whole family would be there. She said that they would all see me after the show.

I waited all day, until Mommy finally said that it was time to go to the arena.

I got ready in the locker room at the arena. I loved my beautiful pink spangly outfit. Mommy even put my hair up in a fancy way. "This is a special occasion," she said.

I looked in the mirror outside the locker room. I looked like a princess. A real skating star.

"Hey, Karen!" Ian said. I turned to look at my partner. Ian's outfit was blue. "Do you like my costume?" he asked.

"You look great, Ian," I said.

"After Roman told me about the outfit that he had to wear at his first performance, I did not think this was so bad. Roman had to wear a costume with feathers, and he sneezed through his whole routine!"

Ian and I laughed as we thought about Roman in a feathered costume.

Soon it was time for the show to begin. Ian and I waited for the pairs part of the program. When it was our turn, we skated out to the center of the ice. I was a little scared. The arena was very dark. Looking out into the audience, it was impossible to see faces. We just heard lots of cheering. I knew that my family and everyone in Ms.

Colman's class were there cheering for us. We just could not see them.

As soon as the music started, I felt better. The familiar count started in my head, and Ian and I began to skate. We did everything perfectly. Our waltz jumps were done at the same time and I even held my leg extension straight. The crowd was cheering, and Ian and I were both smiling. When the music ended, Ian and I skated to the center of the rink. We bowed and then skated off the ice holding hands. We had done it!

Mrs. Harris gave us each a huge hug and told us that we had been perfect. Back in the locker room we saw our friends and families. Ms. Colman was there too. Ian and I each got flowers, stuffed animals, and chocolate! (Nannie made Ian and me chocolate ice skates.)

Mrs. Harris told us that we should go up to the sky box to watch the next performers. "It is a special treat," she said.

We all sat in the large box overlooking the rink. The lights dimmed, and the first few

notes of *Swan Lake* played throughout the arena.

"It's Jillian and Roman!" Ian said.

We watched the couple glide across the ice. I was so proud that they were my friends. I smiled at Ian. I knew he was feeling as proud as I was about the skating pair.

When they finished skating, the crowd roared with applause. People even threw flowers on the ice and Jillian and Roman skated around to sweep them up.

"Wow, I would love to be just like Jillian," Nancy said to me. "She makes skating look so easy."

I smiled at Nancy. "She works very hard," I said. "But that is because she really loves to skate and to perform."

I watched my friend out on the ice. Jillian raised her hand that was full of flowers and waved at me. I jumped up and waved at Jillian, a true star skater.

L. GODWIN

About the Author

ANN M. MARTIN lives in New York City and loves animals, especially cats. She has two cats of her own, Gussie and Woody.

Other books by Ann M. Martin that you might enjoy are *Stage Fright*; *Me and Katie (the Pest)*; and the books in *The Baby-sitters Club* series.

Ann likes ice cream and *I Love Lucy*. And she has her own little sister, whose name is Jane.

Little Sister

Don't miss #119

KAREN'S YO-YO

"I have an idea," I said. I reached into my desk and brought out the Genius. "We can do an experiment." I lowered the Genius a little way down the string and let it swing back and forth. "It is swinging very quickly, like a short pendulum," I observed. Then I let the Genius roll down to the end of the string and swung it gently. "Now that it is a long pendulum, it swings more slowly."

"Hey," said Hannie. "That is great. Now I get it."

"Me too," said Hank.

I smiled. "And all thanks to the Gen — "

"What is that toy doing out, young lady?" snapped a loud, angry voice.

I whirled around. Ms. Holland was standing behind me, with her hands on her hips. "It is my yo-yo. I was just — " I began.

"I can see that it is a yo-yo, and I can see that you are using valuable class time to play with toys." Ms. Holland held out her hand. "Give it to me."

I started to argue. "But I was just showing how a pendu — "

"You were just playing," Ms. Holland interrupted. "Now hand it over."

BABY-SITTERS™

Little Sister

by Ann M. Martin
author of The Baby-sitters Club®

❑	MQ44300-3	#1	Karen's Witch	$2.95
❑	MQ44258-9	#5	Karen's School Picture	$2.95
❑	MQ43651-1	#10	Karen's Grandmothers	$2.95
❑	MQ43645-7	#15	Karen's in Love	$2.95
❑	MQ44823-4	#20	Karen's Carnival	$2.95
❑	MQ44831-5	#25	Karen's Pen Pal	$2.95
❑	MQ44830-7	#26	Karen's Ducklings	$2.95
❑	MQ44829-3	#27	Karen's Big Joke	$2.95
❑	MQ44828-5	#28	Karen's Tea Party	$2.95
❑	MQ44825-0	#29	Karen's Cartwheel	$2.75
❑	MQ45645-8	#30	Karen's Kittens	$2.95
❑	MQ45646-6	#31	Karen's Bully	$2.95
❑	MQ45647-4	#32	Karen's Pumpkin Patch	$2.95
❑	MQ45648-2	#33	Karen's Secret	$2.95
❑	MQ45650-4	#34	Karen's Snow Day	$2.95
❑	MQ45652-0	#35	Karen's Doll Hospital	$2.95
❑	MQ45651-2	#36	Karen's New Friend	$2.95
❑	MQ45653-9	#37	Karen's Tuba	$2.95
❑	MQ45655-5	#38	Karen's Big Lie	$2.95
❑	MQ45654-7	#39	Karen's Wedding	$2.95
❑	MQ47040-X	#40	Karen's Newspaper	$2.95
❑	MQ47041-8	#41	Karen's School	$2.95
❑	MQ47042-6	#42	Karen's Pizza Party	$2.95
❑	MQ46912-6	#43	Karen's Toothache	$2.95
❑	MQ47043-4	#44	Karen's Big Weekend	$2.95
❑	MQ47044-2	#45	Karen's Twin	$2.95
❑	MQ47045-0	#46	Karen's Baby-sitter	$2.95
❑	MQ46913-4	#47	Karen's Kite	$2.95
❑	MQ47046-9	#48	Karen's Two Families	$2.95
❑	MQ47047-7	#49	Karen's Stepmother	$2.95
❑	MQ47048-5	#50	Karen's Lucky Penny	$2.95
❑	MQ48230-0	#55	Karen's Magician	$2.95
❑	MQ48305-6	#60	Karen's Pony	$2.95
❑	MQ25998-9	#65	Karen's Toys	$2.95
❑	MQ26279-3	#66	Karen's Monsters	$2.95
❑	MQ26024-3	#67	Karen's Turkey Day	$2.95
❑	MQ26025-1	#68	Karen's Angel	$2.95
❑	MQ26193-2	#69	Karen's Big Sister	$2.95
❑	MQ26280-7	#70	Karen's Grandad	$2.95
❑	MQ26194-0	#71	Karen's Island Adventure	$2.95
❑	MQ26195-9	#72	Karen's New Puppy	$2.95
❑	MQ26301-3	#73	Karen's Dinosaur	$2.95
❑	MQ26214-9	#74	Karen's Softball Mystery	$2.95
❑	MQ69183-X	#75	Karen's County Fair	$2.95
❑	MQ69184-8	#76	Karen's Magic Garden	$2.95
❑	MQ69185-6	#77	Karen's School Surprise	$2.99
❑	MQ69186-4	#78	Karen's Half Birthday	$2.99
❑	MQ69187-2	#79	Karen's Big Fight	$2.99

More Titles... ➡

The Baby-sitters Little Sister titles continued...

❏	MQ69188-0 #80	Karen's Christmas Tree	$2.99
❏	MQ69189-9 #81	Karen's Accident	$2.99
❏	MQ69190-2 #82	Karen's Secret Valentine	$3.50
❏	MQ69191-0 #83	Karen's Bunny	$3.50
❏	MQ69192-9 #84	Karen's Big Job	$3.50
❏	MQ69193-7 #85	Karen's Treasure	$3.50
❏	MQ69194-5 #86	Karen's Telephone Trouble	$3.50
❏	MQ06585-8 #87	Karen's Pony Camp	$3.50
❏	MQ06586-6 #88	Karen's Puppet Show	$3.50
❏	MQ06587-4 #89	Karen's Unicorn	$3.50
❏	MQ06588-2 #90	Karen's Haunted House	$3.50
❏	MQ06589-0 #91	Karen's Pilgrim	$3.50
❏	MQ06590-4 #92	Karen's Sleigh Ride	$3.50
❏	MQ06591-2 #93	Karen's Cooking Contest	$3.50
❏	MQ06592-0 #94	Karen's Snow Princess	$3.50
❏	MQ06593-9 #95	Karen's Promise	$3.50
❏	MQ06594-7 #96	Karen's Big Move	$3.50
❏	MQ06595-5 #97	Karen's Paper Route	$3.50
❏	MQ06596-3 #98	Karen's Fishing Trip	$3.50
❏	MQ49760-X #99	Karen's Big City Mystery	$3.50
❏	MQ50051-1 #100	Karen's Book	$3.50
❏	MQ50053-8 #101	Karen's Chain Letter	$3.50
❏	MQ50054-6 #102	Karen's Black Cat	$3.50
❏	MQ50055-4 #103	Karen's Movie Star	$3.99
❏	MQ50056-2 #104	Karen's Christmas Carol	$3.99
❏	MQ50057-0 #105	Karen's Nanny	$3.99
❏	MQ50058-9 #106	Karen's President	$3.99
❏	MQ50059-7 #107	Karen's Copycat	$3.99
❏	MQ43647-3	Karen's Wish Super Special #1	$3.25
❏	MQ44834-X	Karen's Plane Trip Super Special #2	$3.25
❏	MQ44827-7	Karen's Mystery Super Special #3	$3.25
❏	MQ45644-X	Karen, Hannie, and Nancy	
		The Three Musketeers Super Special #4	$2.95
❏	MQ45649-0	Karen's Baby Super Special #5	$3.50
❏	MQ46911-8	Karen's Campout Super Special #6	$3.25
❏	MQ55407-7	BSLS Jump Rope Pack	$5.99
❏	MQ73914-X	BSLS Playground Games Pack	$5.99
❏	MQ89735-7	BSLS Photo Scrapbook Book and Camera Pack	$9.99
❏	MQ47677-7	BSLS School Scrapbook	$2.95
❏	MQ13801-4	Baby-sitters Little Sister Laugh Pack	$6.99
❏	MQ26497-2	Karen's Summer Fill-In Book	$2.95

Available wherever you buy books, or use this order form.

Scholastic Inc., P.O. Box 7502, Jefferson City, MO 65102

Please send me the books I have checked above. I am enclosing $_____
(please add $2.00 to cover shipping and handling). Send check or money order – no
cash or C.O.Ds please.

Name_____ Birthdate_____

Address_____

City_____ State/Zip_____

Please allow four to six weeks for delivery. Offer good in U.S.A. only. Sorry, mail orders are not available to residents of Canada. Prices subject to change.   BSLS998